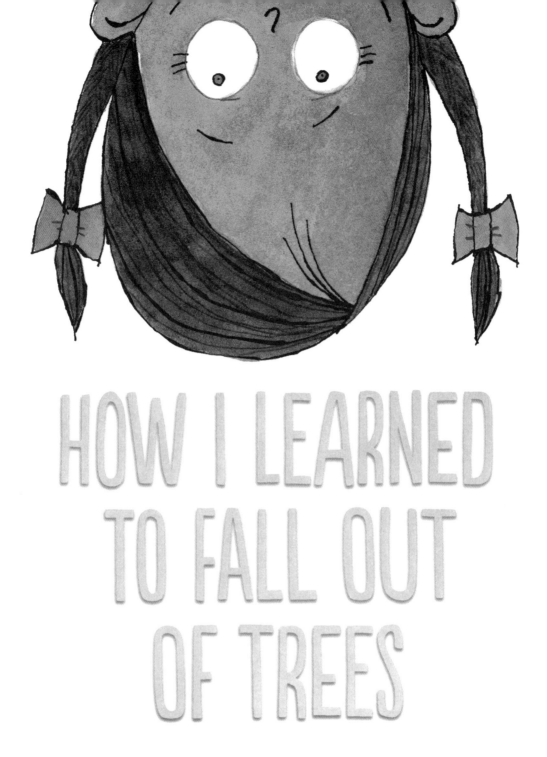

HOW I LEARNED TO FALL OUT OF TREES

Vincent X. Kirsch

Abrams Books for Young Readers • New York

The art in this book was created with watercolor,
Black Star ink/black gesso, all-purpose flat glue, graphite, and cut tracing
paper on hot press illustration watercolor paper.

Library of Congress Cataloging-in-Publication Data:

Names: Kirsch, Vincent X., author, illustrator.
Title: How I learned to fall out of trees / by Vincent X Kirsch.
Description: New York: Abrams Books for Young Readers, [2019] | Summary:
Roger and Adelia have been best friends for many years, so when it is
time for Adelia to move away she plans a special parting gift for him.
Identifiers: LCCN 2018009607 | ISBN 9781419734137 (hardcover with jacket)
Subjects: | CYAC: Best friends—Fiction. | Friendship—Fiction. | Moving,
Household—Fiction. | Tree climbing—Fiction.
Classification: LCC PZ7.K6383 How 2019 | DDC [E]—dc23

Copyright © 2019 by Vincent X. Kirsch
Book design by Julia Marvel

Printed and bound in China
10 9 8 7 6 5 4 3 2 1

Abrams Books for Young Readers are available at special discounts when
purchased in quantity for premiums and promotions as well as fundraising
or educational use. Special editions can also be created to specification. For
details, contact specialsales@abramsbooks.com or the address below.

Abrams® is a registered trademark of Harry N. Abrams, Inc.

ABRAMS The Art of Books
195 Broadway, New York, NY 10007
abramsbooks.com

For Jim

When Adelia told me she
had to move away, she was
up in her favorite tree.

Adelia started collecting
all the soft things
she could find.

She collected
things we secretly
discovered together.

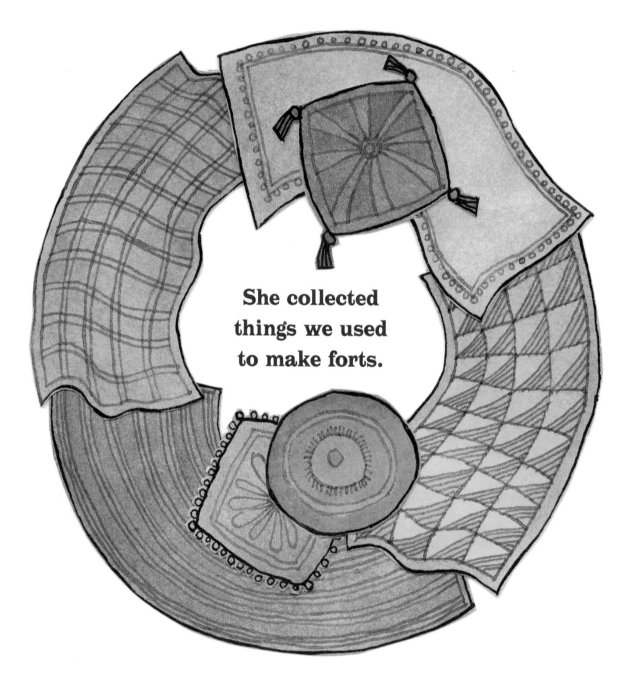

She collected
things we used
to make forts.

She collected
things we loved
to play with.

She collected things
we were supposed
to throw away.

She collected things
we dressed snowmen
in every winter.

It was time to
start packing.

On the day Adelia moved away,
I went back to her favorite tree.

Climbing it was easy.

Letting go was not.

Adelia made certain
that falling was
the easiest part of all.